The Gypsy Witch

Roberta Kagan

Writing as

Veronika Knight

"I always enjoy hearing from my readers. Your feelings about my work are very important to me. Please contact me via Facebook or at www.RobertaKagan.com. All emails are answered personally, and I would love to hear from you."

For a people
whose blood
run's through
my veins and

Whose spirit
lives within my
heart...The
Rom.

Chapter One

"The time for secrets has ended. I can no longer protect you. I am dying."

Tired, her bones visible in her disease-ravaged body, the woman reached for her daughter's slender hand, remembering when hers had been small and delicate.

"Mother stop talking that way, you're not going to die...please"

"Shhh child, quiet, the time has come to listen."

Outside the autumn leaves covered the ground in a blanket of rich burgundy, burnt umber and pumpkin orange. The sun peeked through the already sparse trees shedding light across the earth.

Smiling, the woman began.

"I suppose the best place to start is at the beginning. My family was Lowara Gypsies. Although I was born in Romania, we traveled all across Eastern Europe and Russia. My father was a famous horse trader, quite well known amongst our people.

The summer I was thirteen, we were in Russia on our way up through Siberia. With the harsh winter past, the flat land was covered in dense green forest. A group of young Arabian stallions, which my father hoped to acquire a good sum for, trotted along, hitched to the back of our wagon.

My father had a very fancy vurdun (a gypsy covered wagon that the gypsies use to travel around in) that was painted candy apple red with gold trim and pulled by two fine black saddle bred horses, the finest that we owned. Their thick manes and tails blew back as the wind ran through our wagon train. When we came into this little peasant village called Pokrovskoye that was right beside the Tura River. Our Kompania (a group of gypsies), consisted of at least fifty wagons.

The gage, which was anybody other than the gypsies, gathered around to watch as we rode in. They distrusted us, these peasants, but we brought color and life into their dull worlds, and so they always waited with excitement for the Romany to come to town. I sat looking out the window as the horses hoofs kicked up the dust. I wore a bright blue and pink dress that fell off my shoulders and full at the bottom. The sun shown brightly and everything was illuminated.

During the day, they shunned the Rom. But at night, the women came for having their fortunes told, and the men gathered about our fires to listen to our violin music and watch the gypsy girls dancing.

Unlike some of the peasant villages we had been through, this one had houses. There were one and even two story homes beautifully decorated with very fancy carvings.

A gentle breeze caressed my face and the fresh air waltzed through my hair twirling seductively in my curls. Oh, I was quite the looker in those days, like you are now. I had a long thick raven colored mane and a slim but curvy figure, like yours.

In the square, I saw a gathering. I will never forget how I felt when I first saw him. Oh child, he was something to see.

He was talking and waving his arms in the center of a good size crowd, a man of about twenty years. His black hair was long and uncombed, but he didn't seem to notice. And he wore a thick scraggly beard. Even from where I was, I could see the deep, penetrating navy blue of his eyes. His arms flayed about as he was filled with passion and conviction. The very power of the man had a magnetic attraction and I saw it in the faces of all those surrounding him.

I could not hear what he was saying, so I just watched.

My father parked the wagon and I heard the familiar back and forth negotiations for the horses.

That night we made camp on the outskirts of the town right on the river. It was quite lovely because it was July and the night was not too hot.

My extended family lit our fires and began to cook. The smells were wonderful, as we always had fresh food. Many times, it was stolen from the local gage, but sometimes it was given to us as gifts. Most of the men were good shots so the abundance of fresh kill was always available. My mouth watered as the pungent aromas of meat on the open fire filled the air. I should mention to you, so that you had better understand your people, that the Roma never kill or take more than they can eat. There is no killing for sport amongst us.

That night, I can still remember it; we ate a meal of hedgehog, a favorite of everyone's. Then we built a large campfire and the women made a rich, strong, coffee with lots of sugar while the men drank brandy. We were joyful just to be alive.

The dancing and music went on late into the night and when exhaustion had took over; we lay our eiderdowns under the stars and slept. When the weather was good, we always spent our nights in the open air. During the winter we settled in one place, rested in our wagons and longed for the time when we would hear our leader the Shero Rom yell "Good Road" and once again we would be traveling.

Perhaps it was 2am when I heard the faint sobbing. I awoke and sat up to see what was going on. There beneath a tree right beside our wagon was the man I had seen earlier in the square. I got up and although it was not really permitted for gypsy girls to have contact with men, I was so fascinated that I walked over to him.

He looked at me and I was glued to the ground by those eyes.

"Sit" he ordered, and I did.

I cannot express to you the power that this man's magnetism held. He commanded and people obeyed. At that time, even I obeyed.

His name was Grigori Rasputin. He was a holy man, he said. Just having returned from a monastery at Verkhoture where he had studied with the Khlysty sect.

I asked him what that was and why he was crying.

He told me that he had seen me when we first pulled into town and he cried for my immortal soul.

I listened fascinated and a little bit terrified too. I had never thought of such things.

In the Khlysty, he said sin could be obliterated through the expending of sexual energy.

Then he took me into his arms. I was weak under his spell. He had a power with women, one that would later serve to destroy him.

I was a virgin, and he was a powerful lover. Need I tell you more?

He ravaged my young body with a passion I could hardly resist.

I gave him my heart that night, and he took it without a thought. As, I would later learn, he had taken the hearts of so many.

What he didn't know, was that I was the "special one" the Zigeuya Chovinhani, the gypsy witch. But he was soon to find out.

Chapter Two

I was born into my magic, but he taught me to use the power of sex to enhance it. I came from a long line of witches. This you must know, you too, my love have the gift and the curse of sorcery.

I could possess anything that I should desire if I were able to hold it in my mind through an entire orgasm. This is what I learned. It is a form of sex magic. Grigori had studied it while traveling to a monastery at Verkhoture where he met a sect called the Khlysty.

I know my daughter that you find this strange that I should tell you such a thing, but it is something that you must know in order to understand what happened later.

Night after night, we met in secret and we loved. How we loved.

When he told me that I could possess anything that I wished for, all I could think of that I had ever truly wanted was he.

As he held me in his arms and we joined together to become as one, the power of his lips devoured me. I was so lost and completely immersed in his touch that I could not perform the sex magic. When he was inside of me, I could concentrate not at all. But still I believe that he came to love me as much as he could love anyone after himself.

Not all magicians or sorcerers have the same abilities. My strengths lie in the power to destroy or protect. I could, I knew, curse an enemy or bless a friend and my harm or protection would have a fierce effect.

Grigori was a healer.

It was in his hands. When he laid them upon someone in need, he could end their ills and suffering.

I watched him once as a dog lay dying upon the street. It had been attacked by a larger animal and it writhed in pain. Dried blood crusted the coat of the poor creature's abdomen.

Grigori rubbed his hands together and began to chant to himself. Then he put his hands gently upon the pup. I watched mesmerized as the animal responded coming back from a near death and walking away in perfect health.

My love for him grew in that moment.

I wanted to marry him. I begged him in fact, because I knew that our Kampania would be leaving Russia before the winter set in and I didn't want to leave without him.

I was only fourteen he was eight years older.

When your family returns next year, we will marry. He told me.

And I believed.

The morning that my father took his seat up at the front of our wagon and as he yelled out to the other families "good road," I watched through the window as Grigori stood on the side of the street. It was a dirt path really and the dust flew up as the horses trotted and the wheels turned and we began our journey out of Russia before the cold weather snapped her icy fingers paralyzing Siberia.

He tipped his hat to me and my heart leapt as we rounded a corner and I could see him no more. Memories of our love hurt deep in my stomach as I thought of his eyes, his skin, and his hair. We were moving at a fast speed now. My parents were singing old folk songs in Romany and all of the families were glad to be traveling again. The mood was festive as it always was when we were moving, but this time I was filled with sadness.

We traveled through Romania and Poland, then through Germany and back again. My father worked the gage in all of the small towns trading horses and my mother read cards. I too read but my heart was still back with Grigori and I had lost my accuracy in fortune telling.

When we came back to Northern Russia and then up through Siberia the following year I was overcome with excitement as I waited to see him.

I was a year older. I studied myself in the mirror and I was pleased to see that I had matured. As we had traveled from town to town I saw how men looked at me as I danced illuminated by the glow of the campfire, and I knew that I was beautiful.

For a week, I could not find him. I searched the entire town but did not speak or ask anyone. Finally, I had reached the end of my patience and so I went into a local tavern, which gypsy girls did not do, and I asked the proprietor if he knew of a man called Grigori Rasputin. The tavern was dark and men sat together on wooden stools drinking vodka. They stared at me and the looks in their eyes told me that they harbored dark thoughts. I shook off the fear that I had allowed into my thinking and I waited for an answer.

Not only did the owner know Grigori, but also he knew his wife and daughter.

I left the establishment in a daze.

Grigori was married.

I stumbled back to my father's vurdun and as the others slept in their eiderdowns under the stars, I stayed inside and cried until I felt that I had no more tears. My throat ached.

I watched through the window until dawn, as the moon spread a light like a silver ribbon upon the flowered blankets strewn across the ground.

Grigori found me the following day.

I wanted to destroy him.

Chapter Three

I always kept a hunting knife secured beneath my blanket.

When I heard him approaching, and I had no doubt that, it was him, I reached beneath the eiderdown and my fingers clutched the cool metal.

As he came closer, my heart beat in rhythm with his footsteps. I had every intention of killing him.

Standing quickly with the knife in my hand, I raised it ready to plunge it deeply into his unfaithful heart.

He saw me coming at him. He did not move, in fact, he didn't flinch. With his right hand, he reached and took hold of my wrist. Fight as I might the knife dropped to the ground. With my fists, I beat upon his chest as hard as I was able. Tears stung my eyes and covered my face, but still I fought. I continued to throw blows at him until he took me into his arms and I smelled that familiar smell of cinnamon that always surrounded him. Now I sobbed aloud in earnest, as I knew that I would betray myself.

I could not resist him. He fixed upon me with those eyes as deep as the bluest ocean I had ever seen and then his lips warm as a sunlit summer day touched upon mine. All fight left my body. I wanted him. How I had longed for him and now, he stood before me.

He knew instinctively how I felt. I could not see, my eyes blurred and the world spun around outside of the circle that became us. I cried out when he entered me, for this time it was different. This time I knew that I would bear his child. I felt the life enter my body as his sperm found my waiting, longing egg. He gave me life and our bodies formed together as one to bring forth another.

After it was over and I lay in his arms, both of us temporarily spent, I asked him why?

He told me that he had married her because he had not believed that I would ever come back. I knew he lied to me, but I wanted to believe him and so I did.

By the end of August, I knew that I was right. My monthly blood had not come for ten weeks. I was with child.

I was sure that my father would be furious. He might tell me to leave his vurdun. After all, I could not bring a good bride price anymore. I was a woman who had been spoiled; no decent man of the Rom would want me now.

Strangely enough, my father cried when he learned of my plight. I almost wished that he would hit me or holler but he didn't. He just stood looking out over the river as we sat on the bank, shaking his head. Tears spilling simply from his eyes like the raindrops in a summer shower. I had hurt him terribly and that was far worse than hurting myself.

"Stay here. I will put you up in a room," Grigori told me when he learned that we were to have a child.

I knew he was married and that I would never be more to him than a whore, but I still chose to stay. It was when my father learned that I would not be moving on with the Kompania, that he became angry. Not at me but at Grigori. He took his pistol and in spite of my pleading, he went off to find my lover.

Fear took over my entire body. I tore at my hair. My mother screamed with worry. If he shot Rasputin, my father would be executed by the gage. We were both sure of this. Sweat poured down the front of my dress as I faced anxiety, as if I had never known. Ashamed I could not face my mama, for it was not my father's well being that concerned me it was Grigori's.

I had no choice but to use my most powerful gift.

And so... with all of the heart that I had, I threw the strongest spell of protection upon Rasputin.

He could not be killed, not as long as the magical blanket I had laid upon him continued to cover him. Only I could lift the spell, and so he was safe.

I was in a room at a cheap hotel when I faintly heard the caravan as it pulled out of town. My father's voice haunted me as unenthusiastically he said "good road." I looked around at the single bed and the tiny well-worn dresser and I knew that I would miss the open road, but not enough to give up what I so adored.

I was so young and so foolish. I could not see beyond my love for this magical man and so for a while I was happy. He came to me at least twice a week and when he was not with me, I knew he was at home with his wife. Somehow, I had become used to her. She no longer bothered me.

When he came, we laughed and we loved. He was very excited that I was with child. I became large and my belly button stuck out. This made him laugh and so it made me laugh also. My breasts were heavy and he said that when the child was born he would drink from one and the baby would nourish itself from the other.

We shared so much joy. I believe that was the happiest time of my life. I prayed that it was to last forever.

But...it was not to be so.

Chapter Four

Alone.

I awakened in a pool of blood.

I was wet and cold, it was December in Siberia. I shivered as the loss of blood combined with the weather took hold.

My head ached and the severe pain I felt in my abdomen was excruciating.

I knew that I had lost the baby.

The possibility that I myself would die crossed my mind for a moment. There was so much blood. It was as if a murder had been committed. The sheets were soaked with it. A rich substance of bright red mixed with a garnet color almost black. Pieces of matter were intermingled with the thick liquid and as I touched them, I wondered if they were parts of my unborn child.

The bile rose in my throat and I had no strength to move so I turned and vomited over the side of the bed.

It's quite strange really; the things that you think about when you feel that perhaps you will die. In delirium, I laughed to myself. Until I had moved into this small room, I had never slept in a bed. The Rom does not sleep on beds and it had taken me a while to adjust. I thought about this and how in the beginning I felt as if I were floating on a cloud. Now I wondered if my tiny fetus floated across the open sky. Perhaps he or she was a traveler by nature, a true Rom. These were the things that danced in my head as I held my uterus and trembled with cold and pain.

I drifted in and out of sleep.

I woke crying several times. Not for the loss of my life, which at the time I was sure was eminent. But for the small innocent, conceived through such love, which now was no more than a bloody mass. I would never hold this tender infant, or suckle it to my breast.

If one could feel the breaking of ones heart, I felt mine.

I fell once again into a fitful sleep. Dreaming of my childhood, I saw my cousins and me riding bareback through an open field. I could smell the fresh cut hay and the odor of horses all around me. Then I was swimming bare breasted under a hot sunny sky in the blue green ocean, salt water on my lips, my hair-hanging wet against the naked skin on my back.

Then I awakened and I longed for Grigori. How I loved him. If I were to die, I prayed that at least I would see him one last time.

Now the bed was drenched. Blood had dried on my legs, back, and had stuck my nightdress to my skin. I wondered when Grigori would return. If it were not soon, I would not be able to say goodbye.

It was by God's good grace that he appeared late that afternoon. By his face, I knew that I looked bad.

He did not speak, but he fell to his knees beside my bed. Seeing him so frightened and humbled touched my heart and moved me in ways I could not explain. In all of my suffering, his anguish hurt me more than my own pain.

It was a great feat, because I was so weak, but I lifted my arm and ran my fingers through his long hair. Then with all of the strength that I could muster, I smiled at him.

He did not smile back, but sobbed openly. I had never seen such a display before.

Laying his hands upon my body, and remaining on his knees he began to rock back and forth.

"Live" he cried out "You must live...I command you to live."

Over and over until his voice became hoarse he continued to chant. The whites of his eyes were all that I could see, the familiar sapphire color had rolled back in his head.

He rocked harder now and his voice bellowed out

"Live, live, live....I give to you the breath of my life...take years from me if you will that she may live."

And I did. Maybe an hour, maybe two passed. I began to feel my strength return. Not all at once, but slowly and steadily.

Grigori was so attentive; he bathed me and changed my bed discarding the bloody linens. With the few vegetables that I had, he prepared a soup and insisted that I eat. Holding the spoon as I slurped.

As if I could have loved him any more than I already did, on that day I felt that my love had grown beyond anything imaginable.

For two solid weeks, he stayed with me, never leaving my side. I thought about his wife, but decided that she must know him as I did. Grigori would not be owned.

Finally, I was feeling better.

I took to reading cards in my room. The peasant women of the town visited me asking for spells. I gave them what they wished and some came to love me.

Of course, I tried every known bit of magic on my own lover, in an effort to make him stay, but nothing worked. I lit candles and tied his hair up with mine encircled with red ribbons, I drank his semen mixed with herbs. I carried a piece of his clothing in my locket, but no love spell could conquer him.

And at the end of two weeks, he left. He was gone for the remainder of the winter. It was during these frigid months that I began to have dreams. In them, I saw white doves flying and being torn to shreds by hawks. The death card in the tarot danced before me, the skeleton jumping off the paper. I woke in a cold sweat. The dreams became longer and more vivid.

I knew something was going to happen.

Chapter Five

BLOOD. BLOOD. BLOOD...

Would I never escape it?

I dreamt one night of a river turning red as ripe pomegranates. The water took on living form and wrapped itself around my neck. I was choking. I was drowning. Coughing, I awoke bending at the waist and trying to catch my breath. My heart pounded as I wiped the sweat from my brow.

Although darkness filled this frigid land, I could find no comfort in sleep.

The days were dismal and sunless, the nights even worse.

Gripped by loneliness, I was haunted with memories of my childhood. I wished that I had the company of one of the dogs that I had been raised with, but alas, I was alone. With Grigori gone, the emptiness became unbearable. Finances, at least, were not a problem; he had left me well cared for.

Outside my window, snow fell over thick coatings of ice. Walking was treacherous. Now I knew why the Gypsies left this place while the summer still prevailed.

That winter was the longest I have ever known.

When a bright spring sun began to show her face, the earth responded in kind. I felt so renewed. Each tiny flower was a breath of life to my weary soul. The deep green leaves and the swaying grass filled my aching heart with joy.

Soon the colorful ballet of spring would be in full force.

In a few months, my parents and the rest of the Kompania would arrive. I had jitters in anticipation. I knew that I had brought shame upon my father. Still, I longed to see him. Even if he were still angry, I would revel in the sound of his voice. How I had missed them.

It was late July before the caravan came through town. The wagons rolled in with a new flock of horses roped on the backs. They planned to trade furiously here in Siberia.

I watched from the street as the wagons rolled along, remembering how I had felt when I was among the travelers.

The horses whinnied and shook their manes, as their shoes clip-clopped along the cobblestone road. The dogs ran chasing each other and barking, along the side of the vudons. From where I stood, I heard the familiar Romany folk songs and my heart melted.

Tears and memories.

Then I saw my parent's wagon, and I knew.

One of the boys from another family sat at the front driving the horses.

Running as fast as I could I follow the wagons out of town to the campgrounds. By the time, I reached my mother I was out of breath. She stood outside stretching. Before she saw me, I took notice of her once long black hair, which was now white. Her slender body slumped over, and the wonderful light that I had known all of my life had left her eyes.

"Mama" She opened her arms and I ran inside like I had done as a child.

"Your father is dead. He died of a broken heart. We were riding along the Big River and he fell over and was dead."

Now I knew what the dreams meant.

I blamed myself.

It was then and there that I decided that when the Kompania left I would be with them. I would drive the wagon and take care of my poor mother for the rest of her days. I owed her that much.

Silently I prayed that Grigori would not return. For if he did, I knew that my resolve would be tested.

Chapter Six

For several years, my mother and I traveled through Europe in our wagon.

I became as good as any man at horse-trading. I could mix up a potion for a tired old animal and when the gage came to look at it the beast acted like a young colt. My mother and I told fortunes and depended on the generosity of the rest of the Kompania. And so we got by.

It was in the countryside in the outskirts of Munich during the height of the strawberry season that my life changed forever.

There were trees filled with white blossoms and flowers growing wild on the sides of the dirt road.

We set up camp by a small stream on a hilly green patch of land. The leafy trees with thick trunks gave us shade from the sun. All around us the gage were tending their farms.

On hands and knees, the peasants picked the ripe fruit and filled their baskets. I saw them as they hurried about, their hands red with juice.

My mother had been weak and ill for a while. But since we had come to the highlands of Germany, her color returned and instead of laying around for most of the day, she was up and around playing with the little ones and talking to the other women.

That night I gathered wood and began to build our cooking fire.

"Do you smell the strawberries?"

"You want some, mama?"

She would not ask me to bargain or steal them from the gage. As she was growing older, she became more frightened. She feared arrest and persecution. In her lifetime, she had certainly seen enough of it. But I thought that perhaps the fresh fruit might improve her condition.

At sunset, under the protective veil of a darkening sky, I set out to get your grandmother some berries.

Exhausted from laboring in the sun, the peasants would be retired for the night, leaving the fields unattended.

For a while, I walked gazing at the farmhouses their lights glowing softly. I wondered about the lives of their inhabitants. Finally, I came upon a patch of land, with a house covered by darkness. Instead of candles, burning in windows with pretty embroidered curtains this one appeared empty. Yet, someone was tending the land, for the fruit grew in perfect rows.

I knelt on the ground and began to pick the ripe berries off the vine. Tasting a morsel, I marveled at how sunshine came through in the gifts mother earth gave us. I sat back, folded my legs beneath me, and savored the sweetness.

For a moment, I forgot I was stealing. I sat there on the ground, my magenta and gold skirts billowing out around me, my shoulders bared as my white blouse fell carelessly about my breasts almost revealing my nipples. A cool breeze came down from the north and caressed my hair, gently floating through my long black curls. I was enjoying the beauty of the approaching night, the taste of the strawberries and the light of the new moon rising. I didn't see him.

He walked over to me, his golden hair falling over his eyes in the moonlight. At first I was frightened. I thought he might call the police. We were gypsies, usually not welcome by the farmers. They knew that we took their crops and they were leery of us.

I felt a rush of blood to my head and my heart began to thump.

Not only was I in terrible danger, but I could bring the law's wrath upon the entire Kompania. I tried to get up and run, but he grabbed my arm.

"Are you stealing?"

I didn't answer. To be honest, I wondered why he was asking me, because the answer was obvious.

He was very tall, and as he spoke, I looked up into his eyes.

Expecting to see rage, I found it strange but I saw the kindness in his face and my fear subsided. He had warmth in his eyes and an openness I'd not seen in a man before, not in the Romany men, and certainly not in Grigori.

Knitting his brow, he shook his head.

"You're hurting my arm."

Suddenly embarrassed, he released me.

"I'm sorry."

Then he crossed his arms over his chest and I could see he felt awkward.

But beneath the false exterior, even in the semi-darkness, I saw the quickest flash of desire come over his face. It was there one moment and then it was gone. I knew in that instant that I had the power to keep him from going to the authorities. After Grigori, I knew how easily men were distracted when sex was involved.

"This is your farm? Then I guess these strawberries are yours."

I probably should have been afraid, but I wasn't. Something told me to go ahead and take the chance.

Looking deep into his eyes, I took a strawberry from the basket, which was now on the ground between us. Then I ran my tongue over the surface and took a bite. I took the rest of the strawberry, the juice dripping down my hand and I walked over to him. Slowly I lifted the scarlet fruit to his lips and rubbed it softly until his mouth opened.

What a fool this man is, I thought to myself, so easily manipulated by an unspoken promise.

After Grigori I was done with all of that.

Or so I thought.

Trying to feign anger, he looked down at me.

"You shouldn't steal."

Then for no reason at all he laughed. His laughter was warm and contagious and I could not help but laugh as well.

"I guess you can't tell a gypsy not to steal."

"And I guess you can't tell a gago to be smart enough to expect it."

He sat down on the ground beside me and began to help me gather strawberries.

"I suppose these are for your poor hungry children?'

"Actually no, they are for my poor sick mother."

"Now, now, you needn't make up stories for me. I welcome you to take my strawberries."

"In fact, it's true. They are for my mother and she has been ill as of late."

"I'm sorry to hear that. Is there no husband who could have come stealing for you?"

"No, I'm sorry to say. I have no husband."

His face lit up brighter than the stars in the sky. A white perfect smile with dimples that made him seems more of a boy than a man.

I had not looked at him before, had not taken notice of the muscles that stood out on his arms and chest, or of the tightness of his flat stomach. Tall and well built, I could see the man had spent his life farming.

I learned he was alone. His parents had died several years earlier and he had lost his wife the previous year in an accident. She had taken her horse and buggy into town and lost control. He told me that he wished he had gone with her, but she had insisted on going alone.

Having experienced the guilt over my father's death, I recognized it in him.

His name was Jan Reinhardt. He was honest, uncomplicated, and kind, with the type of good looks only a gago can have.

And I found I liked him in spite of myself.

Chapter Seven

The outskirts of Munich Germany late 1800's
through early 1900's

Jan surprised me. He was different than I
expected

Every day, after working his land, he came to see
me. And I suppose you could say he courted me.

He always brought gifts. Sometimes, fresh eggs
from his chickens, another time ribbons for my hair,
but he never came without a basket of ripe
strawberries for mama and me.

With his hair blowing softly in the gentle breeze,
crisp black pants, and white cotton shirt, he walked
through the rolling green hillside with me. We were
quite a sight, me, barefoot, with my full skirts and
uncovered shoulders and him with his dimples and
golden hair, falling over his eyes.

Mama openly disapproved.

"Do you realize what everyone is saying about
you?"

"No, mama and I don't care."

"Well, you should. You take walks alone with a man, and not only a man, but he isn't even a Rom. Are you crazy? That's it, maybe you've lost your mind. No decent man of the Rom would have anything to do with you now."

"Mama, please, I have long since given up the idea of marrying. I wouldn't bring much of a bride price anymore. I'm sure that everyone has their own ideas about what happened with Grigori and I. Their tongues were wagging then too, I'm sure."

"Yes, they were, and your poor father, may he rest in peace, was so ashamed."

'Thank you for that information, mama. I never meant to hurt either of you."

"NO, and you don't now either. You just have a very stubborn streak and it costs you and your family dearly. You think that you can do exactly as you please and there aren't going to be any consequences. Well, if you hadn't run off with that straggly lunatic, you would probably be married by now."

"I've admitted that Grigori was a mistake. I've paid the price. What more do you want from me."

"That long dirty hair of his, what were you thinking?'

"Mama, enough about the past and Grigori, this conversation is going nowhere. Jan is on his way, and if you don't mind I'd like to get ready."

"Sure, go ahead. You paid the price alright and you'll pay again with this one. You're gonna see."

Shaking her index finger at me like a knife my mother always knew the perfect words to cut to the core of my being.

At six thirty, Jan arrived as he did every evening. Placing a basket of strawberries on the table, he turned to me and handed me a box of chocolates.

"I went into town to get these for you. I hope you like them"

"Thank you. I'm sure I will."

"Chocolate is no good for your skin" my mother grimaced.

"Thank you for the advice, mama, Jan and I are going out for a walk"

We left.

"Excuse her, she's afraid of you, because you aren't Rom."

"It's okay, I'll win her over. It might take time, but I'll do it." He smiled and I saw those dimples again.

Jan was a good listener, and I had a lot to talk about. It had been so long since I had the luxury of leaning on anyone. I was the one mama depended upon and it was my responsibility to be strong.

I told him, as we sat under a weeping willow tree, how I had learned to trade horses with the gago. Instead of being put off, I saw appreciation in his face. Against better judgment, I invited him to come and eat with my mother and me and then to watch the girls dance at the campfire.

"Will you dance for me?"

"Me? I haven't danced in years."

"Did you forget how?" he winked

"You never forget."

"Then you'll dance for me?"

I couldn't help but laugh. He had this way of looking at me with his head tilted and a twinkle in his eyes that sent a warm glow through my entire body.

The night he came for dinner, I was nervous. I wasn't sure what my mother might say to him, or how the others would treat him. But he didn't care. His eyes never left me. And, for the first time since I met Grigori I joined the girls in the dance. Jan sat with his legs crossed under him and watched me. He never looked at any of the others.

I danced for him.

The violins played the haunting Romany melodies and as I twirled, my china blue skirts floated in waves around my body. My hair was loose and black curls fell about my face as the campfire burned like the passion between Jan and I.

When the rest of the Kompania took their eiderdowns out and laid them under the stars, I took

Jan's hand and led him away. I caught the look of horror on my mother's face, but I did not turn back.

For a mile, we strolled silently hand in hand bathed by the illumination of a full moon. I looked up at the sky and saw a falling star.

"Look quickly, do you see that? It's a falling star. Make a wish, if you do it will come true."

He closed his eyes and I watched him take on a serious expression as he spoke to the dropping silver speck of light.

"Little star it is my wish that you make this woman love me as much as I have come to love her."

He was so genuine. When he looked at blue and me with eyes bright, innocent I felt a slight twinge in my heart.

"I do love you." He said.

I believed him.

For the first time, he kissed me. It was a soft and gentle kiss. Taking me in his arms, I felt the powerful muscles close gently around me enveloping me in a cocoon of strength and safety. His warm lips brushed against mine.

I took his hand and guided him to the ground.

It was I who initiated our lovemaking.

He would never have been so bold. Not because he was weak, but he would never have risked offending me.

I slipped my blouse over my head and let my skirts fall to the ground. Standing naked before him, I saw the desire and admiration in his eyes. I knelt beside him and unbuttoned his shirt. He reached up and caressed my face with a gentle hand. Then I unbuttoned his pants. As light as a breeze, I ran my fingers across his chest and then his stomach. I felt the hard muscles jerk with excitement beneath my hands. I wanted to explore and come to know every part of him.

"You never cease to amaze me." The hoarseness in his voice caused a shiver between my thighs.

I removed his pants and kneeling between his legs I took him into my hands. He was hard and throbbing. Leaning over I allowed my hair to brush his bare thighs. His body quivered. Placing my lips over his erect manhood, I listened as he sighed deeply. Kissing, licking and sucking him almost caused him to lose control.

Lifting me up to his face, he kissed me, looked into my eyes, and then carefully placed me on my back. Deliberately and unrushed, he kissed every inch of my body lingering with his lips and tongue as if I were a fine wine to be savored. Finally, when we joined as one he never closed his eyes.

"I want to look at you. You're the most beautiful woman I've ever seen."

Our bodies moved together in a rhythmic dance of heated passion and when we reached our climax, it was I first and then he just seconds later.

He was a tender, considerate lover. I felt as if my body were being worshiped. To him I was a Goddess, and he made sure I knew it.

When it was over, he held me for a long time running his hand through my hair.

"Marry me. I love you more than I ever thought I could love anyone or anything. I realize we might have a difficult time, but I'm willing to fight for you, you're worth it. I'll win your mother, and your people, and mine will accept they or us can be damned. You're everything I have ever wanted."

I felt the tears begin to well in the back of my eyes.

"Jan, before I can say yes, there is something that I must tell you. Once you know you might change your mind, you may not want to have anything to do with me.

"I doubt that. There is nothing that you could tell me that would ever change how I feel about you."

"Before you say that, perhaps, you should listen."

Chapter Eight

My temples pounded and I felt dizzy like I'd gotten up too quickly after lying down for a long time. I had to tell him. Finally, I might have a good life, a husband, perhaps children. With all of this at stake, I could have chosen to keep my secrets, but what kind of marriage would we have? No, I decided, as it became difficult to take a deep breath, he had always been truthful with me so he deserved honesty. So, I would let the cards fall where they may.

"Jan," I swallowed hard, my throat as rough as sand, "there was another man before you."

"Who was he?"

"He was a healer. Some called him the mad monk because of his wild eyes and black robes that he wore. I met him when my family traveled through Siberia."

"Did you love him?"

"I was so very young," I licked my lips pleading, praying he would understand "and he was powerful, much older and persuasive."

I dropped my head, I could not look at him, I could not bear to see the pain I knew would be in his face. Instead, I ran my fingers over the fabric of my skirts, twisting the cotton in my sweaty hands. "I became pregnant, and because of it, for a while, I left the Kompania."

I told him everything, all of it. It felt like my heart had opened and my life's blood was pouring out. In a small voice, barely audible, I explained how Grigori had been like a drug to me. He possessed me.

Jan listened quietly as I divulged the powers I had and the spell I cast on Grigori to keep him safe from danger. Because of his way of living, he had many enemies. I could not heal, or protect him from disease, but as long as he carried my blessing, he could not be murdered.

I went on to tell him about losing the baby and the terrible dark winter when Grigori left me alone. I described that small empty room in Siberia where the walls felt as if they would cave in on me, and the frigid cold and endless loneliness I suffered. And then I told him about the guilt I felt for bringing shame upon our family and causing the death of my father.

In the moonlight, his eyes looked glassy as if he were going to cry. Beneath me, the dew on the grass felt cold although it was a warm night. I felt a shiver rise up the back of my neck and run its icy finger through my hair. I was sure I had lost him. Why would a man want a woman who was so tarnished?

Without a word, he got up. My heart was pounding so hard I was afraid I would vomit. I thought that he would walk away leaving me alone to endure this life I had made for myself, but he didn't. He came to me and took me in his arms. Tears of joy mingled with tears of regret and of relief spilled down my face washing away the anguish, and for the first time in my life I felt safe. I sobbed in his arms and his tenderness allowed me to do so. I had never said this before, to anyone.

"I love you."

"Oh God, that is all I've ever wanted in life. I love you more than I ever loved anyone. You are more precious to me than everything that I own. More precious than my life."

He began kissing me and once again, we lay together.

When I told my mother that Jan and I planned to marry, she was furious.

"So, he's gonna give up his farm and he's gonna move into our wagon with us?"

"No mama, I'm gonna move on to his farm and you're welcome to come and live with us."

"You would do this to me? You would make me live under his roof, and I'm gonna be obligated to him?"

"No, I'm not going to make you do anything. Jan was nice enough to offer to take to you in; if you don't want to come, that's your choice. I can find one of the other families to take you along with them."

"Such a headstrong girl. What a terrible curse. How did you get this bad? Before you met that slob you weren't so ornery."

"Mother, I'm not. But, I love Jan and I want to marry him. Please try to understand that you cannot control my life the way you could papa."

"Oh if your father were alive, you would never treat me like this. No...not if he were here. But since I'm nothing but a lonely widow, you think...ehh...so what...I leave my mother behind to fend for herself. She's old she won't live long. She...."

"Mama, you're driving me crazy. I want you to live with us."

"That gago doesn't...just look at him with that blond hair. Oh, what did I ever do to deserve such a terrible child? Why could you not be like the other girls? Marry a nice Romany boy; bring a hefty bride price so that your old parents could live in luxury. No, you run off with a madman, and instead of a bride price you bring shame. My only child, when you were born I had such hopes for you. Such dreams, and you were so pretty any boy from any Kompania would have been proud to be your husband. But what do you do? You..."

"That's it, that's enough. I'm going outside to wait for Jan."

My mother was difficult but he won her over. In fact, by the time Jan and I were to be married, I think she liked him better than she liked me.

Mama insisted that we marry among the gypsies, and Jan did not protest. My happiness was his greatest concern and he learned the Romany ways, taking to them as if he had been born one of us.

On the day that we were to marry, I woke before dawn. Sitting in the gray cool of the morning, I sipped strong sweet coffee. As the sky turned a light orange and then a soft blue, I thought about how lucky I was to have found such a wonderful man. I must admit, my thoughts did drift to Grigori. I wondered if he still held that terrible mesmerizing power over me, and prayed I would never see him again. I did not trust myself; I did not want to find out what might happen.

With a smile on her face, Mama stretched awake under the shade of a weeping willow tree.

"Ah, what an auspicious day! Look, over there, you see the blue bird? Look, look, quickly... Good luck, yeah?"

"Yes mama, it is. And I feel so lucky, so very fortunate."

"Well, make sure you don't do anything to ruin this do you, understand?"

"Of course, mama."

Even when she was happy, it took every ounce of patience I had to tolerate her comments.

"Come into the vurdun with me. I have something for you."

I knew what it was. I had longed to wear mama's wedding dress since I was a little girl. It was a rich red satin that fell off my shoulders and then tight at my small waist with the fullest skirts you can imagine billowing out all around me.

When she was, a girl mama was thin as I was now, and I knew the dress would fit perfectly. Most Romany girls only wear red on their wedding day, but I loved the color and, against my parent's wishes, I wore it often. It offset my pale skin and raven hair. I tried the dress on and my mother gasped as tears came to her eyes.

"You are so beautiful. My beautiful daughter on her wedding day. Your father is here in spirit. I wish he were with us to marry you."

"It's okay, mama. Uncle Fonso will do it for papa. He is papa's closest brother."

"Your girlfriends have the twigs, water, and bread ready?"

"Of course mama. You know how Lala is, always taking over and making sure things are right. Tsura will do whatever Lala tells her. Don't worry; the girls have everything we need."

"The sea salt, the cup, the bucket, the knife, the cord. There is so much to remember."

"Mama relax, it will be fine. You're making me nervous. I set up the bread and the sea salt. I will go to the river and fill the bucket now." Although she was anxious, I could see in her face how excited and happy she was.

Much to my surprise, Jan arrived early to see my mother. He gave her a brooch that had belonged to his grandmother, a lovely gold butterfly with sparkling sapphire chips inlaid in its wings. For me he gave me his mother's pearls.

Mama came in proudly carrying the gifts. "Look what my new son in law brought for us."

My necklace was magnificent. White as a Siberian virgin snow, the pearls lay on my collarbone showing off the brightness of my smile.

Mama wore her gift with pride and for the first time since I had run off with Grigori she held her head up amongst the other women.

As my uncle explained the meaning of the bond of marriage and snapped the tree branches, I glanced over at Jan. He looked so filled with love and so proud to be my husband that my heart melted.

My best friend Tsura walked over to the wedding wagon and came back with the traditional bag of sea salt, loaf of bread and bucket of water. My cousin Bo took the cup from his pocket and handed it to my uncle who filled it. Uncle Fanso handed the challis to me and then to Jan. We both drank and then setting it on to the ground, with his foot Jan pushed the cup deep into the earth.

I smiled over at my new husband as my uncle gave us each a piece of the bread, then he sprinkled the remainder over our heads and over the ground.

Now came the part that I had always dreaded, the joining of the blood. Lala handed a sterling silver knife decorated with amethyst to my uncle who made a thin cut in Jan's arm. He did not flinch, but I closed my eyes and gritted my teeth as I received my slash. Then as was the custom, our wrists were bound together with a white silk cord that was knotted three times. For fertility, my uncle said as he tied, for consistency, and long life.

As I looked into his face, Uncle Fanso looked so much like my papa that I felt a teardrop down my cheek and wet the bodice of my dress. Handing each of us the sea salt we were instructed to throw a handful over our left shoulders. Then the blood stained cord was removed and cut into two pieces, one given to each of us. "You must keep this string for two years and if you should ever choose to divorce you must bring this with you."

By the look, I saw on Jan's chiseled face and the way that my heart skipped a beat, I didn't think that divorce could ever be possible.

The previous day deep pits had been dug for the fires that would prepare the wedding feast. Food was plentiful; there was roasted hedgehog, rabbit, and chicken. On a spit, someone was barbecuing a whole pig. Potatoes, carrots, and cabbage boiled with garlic in a large cauldron. The men drank our special homemade whiskey, brandy, and beer. Many of the women drank as well. There was the traditional coffee, and the violins played.

Friends of my family gave us gifts of money. They came over, kissed us, and offered their blessings then they handed us cash and said as is our custom. "Here is a little bit of money from me, Let God give you all that you could ever want."

We graciously thanked them. Jan hugging them like a true Rom, as he drank with the men and I saw how they accepted him into our world. I knew the Rom and how they think. Jan would always be a gago, but he was a special one and they liked him.

The party lasted until we were exhausted, and then as was the tradition, Jan and I went off alone. This was the time I was supposed to be losing my virginity.

Our first time as man and wife could not have been any more glorious. The love that radiated from our union filled our marriage bed with joy, such as I had never known.

Mama and I moved to the farm and stored our wagon in the barn.

Sometimes in the afternoon, I could distract Jan from his work and we would take the horses out for a run. He rode with a saddle and I rode bareback as the Rom do. Up we galloped through the hills laughing until we reached the top. I would pack a lunch of cheese and bread and we would stop and eat. Our love was always overcoming us and we found ourselves in each other's arms.

I had a lot to learn about life on a farm. Jan taught me to milk a cow, and we both laughed when the milk sprayed in my face and it trickled down the bodice of my dress. He lifted me off the little stool and picked me up easily, his arms were so strong, then embracing, and we kissed. Tenderly he began to lick the milk that had spilled across my neck and chest. I giggled like a young girl and he laughed.

In the middle of the afternoon, in the barn, lying on a pile of freshly cut hay, he kissed my breasts until we were both so filled with passion we could not stop long enough to get back to the house. Instead, our love consumed us right where we were. With one hand, he reached under my skirts and touched me. I moaned, I was ready, longing to feel his hardness deep inside me.

Jan would not be rushed. He was a slow passionate lover who played my body like a fine Stradivarius. Kissing my thighs with his soft warm lips he slipped his tongue inside of me. My insides caressed him lovingly. Finally, when I could no longer stand to be without him, I begged, and he entered me. And once again, we drifted off to heaven.

Jan was always kind and generous to mama, but not only to us and me. He was a good neighbor. He helped the old farmer who lived down the road, simply because he had no sons of his own. And as Jan told me, the old man was getting on in years and this hard work was too much for him.

The farm consumed our every waking moment. The winter would be comfortable if we prepared now. I learned to make cheese, and to can fruits in glass jars as well as the asparagus that we grew by using heat.

We slaughtered a pig before the winter set in and preserved   the   meat   with   salt. What remained of our crop, Jan took into town and traded or sold to buy grains. There was a cellar under the barn where we stored all of our food. The winter would be easy on us we would have plenty. And, where I had once dreaded the winter, I now longed to spend the cold months warm in Jan's strong embrace.

"Mother" Jan would ask her "What price do you think these asparagus will bring at the market?" He always asked her opinion, always making her feel very important and needed.

"Mother, from the look of the sunset, do you think   we   will   have   rain   tomorrow?" Or "Mother, what do the cards say, will we have a grandchild for you to bounce on your knee before the next year is out?"

She loved it. And, as was his intention, she loved him. I don't think she missed the open road for one minute.

I was happy that they got on so well. My mother had long since stopped telling fortunes for the gage and so did I, but she always read for Jan. She told him how bright our future would be, and he sat and listened, looking very serious, and pretending to believe every word she said.

Mama was taken in. He was her son now, blond and gage or not. It no longer mattered to her. I was happy, for the first time in my life. Every day I saw the miracles in all the small things I had never paid attention to before. The sunsets looked a little pinker and in the morning, the songs of the birds were sweeter. I laughed at the squirrels as the chased each other up and down the thick trunks of the trees.

As I passed the barn, I heard Jan singing and it made me smile.

Whenever Jan went into town, he returned with gifts for mama and me. She was like a gago child at Christmas waiting in eager anticipation for whatever trinket he might bring. Many times, I gathered wild flower bouquets of royal purples, vivid pinks and egg yoke yellows, but quite often, he brought them to the house presenting them to me with a kiss.

Our lives were good. Our lives were very good. Until Grigori found me.

I was on my way back to the house from the chicken coop. I'd been gathering eggs. Jan was in town and mama was asleep. And there he was, his long black robe encircling him with darkness. His hair hung about his shoulders in knots.

"I've finally found you. I have spent the last two years in search. I realized that I love you, and I never want to be apart again." He was walking towards me, his arms outstretched.

My blood ran cold, what was I to do? What, was I ever to do?

Chapter Nine

Damn your soul to hell, Grigori Rasputin. How did you find me? And why in God's name have you come back after so many years?"

I glared into his hypnotic eyes the color of sapphires, terrified of the power he might still have over me.

"I love you, I realized how much."

"And so, you come here and find me with no thought of how this might affect my life?'

"I hoped you would be happy to see me."

He was walking slowly towards me; those eyes never wavered from penetrating my own.

I shook my head.

"No, Grigori, I am not happy to see you. I've been married for a little over two years, happily married."

"Sweet gypsy girl, there is no man for you but me."

He put his arms around me. I felt bile rise up in my throat. I swallowed hard to keep from vomiting.

"No, Grigori"

He did not stop. He would not listen. The basket of eggs dropped from my hand as he knocked me to the ground. Tears filled my eyes. His face-hardened with determination as he attempted to kiss me. With all of my strength, I tried to push him away, but he was incredibly powerful. Using both hands, he grabbed my face pressing his lips hard against mine. Turning quickly away, I spit the taste of his foul kiss from my mouth. Grabbing my shoulders in his massive hands, he shook me hard, at the same time nuzzling into my neck. I reached over and bit his upper arm, the salt of his blood bitter on my tongue. My feet made contact with his legs and groin as I kicked frantically and hammered at his back with my fists. Unable to face what was happening to me, I turned away. There on the ground were the broken eggs and the little white basket lying on its side.

Tears spilled down my face.

With his legs, he forced my thighs open. I fought harder, but he pinned my arms down as he forced himself inside of me. Then glaring into my eyes he began to move and the power of his magic came over me like a black veil and I am ashamed to admit, I wanted him.

I lay beneath him, our eyes fixed together until it was over.

"I told you that you still loved me."

Then he got up and turned to leave. I still lay on the ground my skirts up above my waist and my arms bruised where he had held them.

"I will be back, and when I come I will take you with me."

And he was gone.

The broken eggs had spilled their contents all over the emerald grass. I looked at the mixture of deep yellow and bright green and I vomited.

Back at the house, I agonized. I knew that when he came for me, I would follow Grigori.

I was under his spell.

That evening when Jan returned, I could not sleep beside him. The innocence of his kisses filled me with guilt. I knew what I must do.

In the middle of the night as Jan and mama slept, I went to the barn. I took Mara, my favorite horse, and prepared her for the journey. I gently slipped the bit into her cooperative mouth and pulled the bridle over her head. Jumping onto the animal's bare back, I leaned forward and patted her neck. The smell of horse manure filled the barn. I smoothed her mane and cooed over the side of her ear. Then in the blackest of night, I rode away from all of the happiness I had ever known, to find the only person I thought might be able to break this spell.

I searched the trees in the darkness for patrin, signs that gypsies leave for each other, but found none. Exhausted and blinded by the lack of light from the new moon, I continued to search. Finally, the following morning, I found marks on a bush indicating a Kompania had come through the area. It could be any one of a dozen different groups.

Now there were marks every few yards and I followed them carefully. At one point, I rode through an open field. All around me there were deep purple flowers and a heady sweet fragrance that I found intoxicating. Finding myself lost in the peaceful beauty allowed me for a moment to forget my predicament.

I didn't see them. Three peasant boys of maybe sixteen years were pursuing me on horseback. I might have remained oblivious until they were upon me had one not cried out

"Zigeuya"

They were taunting me. All three of them had fire orange hair, and that made me think that they might be brothers. I had learned to ride early and my horse and I were as one. With a clucking sound as I leaned into her neck. I gave her our signal to pick up speed.

"Go Mara, hurry up girl"

The little horse threw her head back and whinnied as we whipped through the field and across an open dirt road. They were hot on my trail, but they couldn't catch me. Now the boys were hollering as their laughter pierced the air.

"Gypsy girl, come over here. Come on Zigeuya, tell our fortune, we won't hurt you." Wildly they kicked their horses racing each other as much as they were trying to catch me. I knew they meant me no good, learning early in life that boys in a group could spell danger. I turned my horse and rode up a hill and out of the clearing. I ducked back into the forest and road through tight openings in the trees until my horse and I were virtually lost to the gagos.

After a sigh of relief, I patted Mara, grateful for her help, and rode on.

Just as the sun was making her magnificent exit in shades of bright fuchsia calmed by brushstrokes of royal blue, I came upon the kompania. There just a few miles from the Swiss border, a band of gypsy vurduns had stopped for the night.

Dogs were barking as I dismounted, but I was immediately greeted and recognized as Rom. This was not my Kompania, but all gypsies are cousins

"Please, I need to see the Shuvani, the medicine woman. I need help." The two young boys that greeted me were Chavvis, Romany children, and so they understood immediately.

"Come and follow."

They led me to a wagon made of logs, and badly in need of paint.

"In here" One of the boys indicated, and I entered.

A woman sat on the floor her legs splayed out in front of her, white hair caught up in a bun at the nape of her neck; she made a sucking sound as she puffed a silver pipe. Lined like a map, her weathered brown face showed no emotion. But her deep onyx eyes studied me.

"You're in trouble, child."

"Yes, mother. A great deal of trouble."

"Sit then. Tell me."

I told her everything, and she listened as I wept. Then shaking her head she looked into my eyes. The smoke burned my eyes and made me cough as a gray fog floated out of the wide mouth of her pipe each time she inhaled. She rocked back and forth, as she contemplated my situation. Finally, after what seemed like hours, but in fact was only minutes, she placed her pipe on the ground. Only a few teeth remained on either side of her wrinkled mouth, her parched lips smiled in sympathy.

"I will help you. But you know child, you are a gypsy witch as I am. You are a special one. As you grow older, your powers will become stronger. I know you don't believe me, but you have the power to do this yourself if you so chose."

"Old mother, I have some magical abilities, I know, but not against him. He is so strong. I cannot get away. It is essential that the spell be broken, and that he no longer is able to control me. I wish for him to go from my life and leave me in peace."

She continued to rock. Lifting her pipe she stuffed it full again and lit it then continued puffing deeply in silence.

"If you do not believe that you can do it alone, you will not be able to."

Finally, she rose and walked over to a cabinet. She took a bottle of herbs and mixed them with a liquid. "Take this sweet child, and by tomorrow, you will be free of his magic."

Kneeling she handed me the vial. For an old woman she was very limber.

I drank the potion, and felt nothing.

"Old mother, I would like to give you some money."

I took a small velvet purse filled with coins and put it on the floor beside her.

"Do not leave me money, you are Rom, you are one of us."

"But I can spare it and I wish to make this gift to you."

With gnarled fingers, she took the moneybag, and nodded her thanks.

"Hurry home, your husband is filled with worry. Go now, and all will be as you wish."

"Thank you, thank you mother"

Turning away, she dismissed me, then lifted her hand and waved to indicate that our time together was over.

I left.

Through the forest, I rode the sound of galloping hoofs were all I heard. The tree branches scraped my face and arms but I continued faster than an arrow flies.

When I arrived the following morning, Jan skin was the color of the old mother's smoke. I could see by the dark thick swellings beneath his eyes that he had not slept.

"Where were you? I was so worried?'

"Please, don't ask me. I had to go and find a Kompania."

"For what? Couldn't you have waited? I would have gone with you. I found the horse gone and I knew you'd ridden off somewhere. When I thought of you all alone in the dark night, I was distraught. I rode all around town looking, but I couldn't find you. I tore my hair out hoping it was not something I had done. My God, please don't ever do anything like this again."

"It's nothing you did. I walked over and touched his face. I felt him melt like butter.

"Promise me; please that you won't ever do anything like this again."

"I'm so sorry, I won't. I promise."

After riding all night, I was dirty and spent. I bathed my body and my hair. As I lay immersed in the hot soapy water, I was thankful that Jan had not pressed me for more information. I retired to my bed and slept for two days.

I awoke to find Jan beside me, asleep in a chair. Rising from the bed, I walked over to him. Tenderly kissing his cheek, I helped him to lie down. I placed a light blanket over him and he fell asleep. For a few minutes, I stood watching him, filled with tenderness.

Late that afternoon, while Jan was finishing work on the land, Grigori appeared.

"I was here several days ago, looking for you, where have you been?'

"Never mind where I've been. Don't come here anymore."

"You will come with me?"

"No, Grigori, it's over. Leave me in peace. Go."

He started towards me, but his eyes lost their magnetism and I lifted my fingers pointing them at him in the sign of a gypsy curse.

"It's over."

Above us a melody sprung from the throat of a songbird. I saw the fear in his eyes as he looked at my hand. Turning away, Grigori walked quietly out of my life.

I was sure that everything would be fine now. Jan and I would resume our happy marriage, and all would be well. And it was.

For six weeks.

Two events would take place that would change things forever.

Chapter Ten

I was in the kitchen chopping potatoes when I heard mama cry out. Dropping the knife, I ran to see what was wrong. On the wooden floor beside her bed she lay trembling, her face shrouded by a dark shadow.
"What is it Mama?" I knelt beside her.

"I am so dizzy. My head hurts. I am seeing two of everything."

I helped her up and back into bed. Then I ran to the kitchen to boil a pot of water and added a bit of chopped willow bark. The medicine simmered as I cut a chunk of her hair and then ran outside to bury it.

Upon returning, I propped her up with pillows and spooned the mixture into her mouth. Unable to swallow the liquid dribbled from her formless lips, and her face seemed to sag drastically on one side.

"Mama, what can I do?"

"Go and get Jan."

I ran outside to find Jan brushing one of the horses in the barn. He looked up as I entered.

"What's wrong?"

"Mama is sick. She wants you."

"I'm coming."

He followed me back to the house. "I'm here, Mama. What hurts you?"

She told him, and he motioned that I meet him outside the room.

When we were, alone he looked at me gravely.

"I think she's very ill. Perhaps I should go and fetch a doctor."

"Mama would never agree to a gago doctor."

"She might if I talked to her."

"No. I gave her some willow bark and buried a piece of her hair. That should help."

His hand caressed my face."Sweetheart, my love, I know you believe in all of this, but perhaps a doctor might help."

"You insult me."

"Never! I just want what's best for mama."

"I know what's best for mama."

Young and stubborn, I walked away from him. Within days my mother had become an old woman, left eye drooping down exposing the raw inside of her lower lid. Not willing to admit I'd been wrong, I decided I would go into town and find the gago doctor myself. Perhaps, I thought his medicine magic was stronger than my own.

Diligently at work, trying to harvest our crops before the first frost, Jan did not see me as I rode away on horseback.

The cool breeze felt morning fresh on my face, and the sweet smell of harvest permeated the air. Leaves of burgundy and orange crunched beneath her feet, as I maneuvered my horse along the trail into town.

When I arrived, people scurried about. Two men dressed in fancy suits leaned against a wagon wheel, their jaws fat with tobacco as they chomped. With hands, flaying about they negotiated a sale. Hurried along with purpose, ladies dressed in cotton frocks with fancy hats carried baskets of colorful fabric and ribbons. Vendors of all shapes and sizes populated the streets offering fresh fruits and vegetables, along with livestock. The luscious smell of fresh bread wafted out the open door of a bakery. Because I had never learned to read, the signs were meaningless to me. Pacing the streets, I wondered how I would ever find the doctor.

Two of the red-haired boys who had followed me relentlessly when I had gone to see the medicine woman, stood munching on apples outside of a candy store. As they glanced over at me, I noticed them whisper to each other as their eyes narrowed. Being outsmarted by a gypsy angered them. One crossed the street and came towards me. A chill ran up the back of my neck and in an effort to get back to my horse I picked up my pace. Out of an alleyway the other boy came walking towards me, at his side a heavyset police officer sauntered along.

"This good for nothing gypsy stole a chicken from my brother and me." He said, pointing just inches from my face with his index finger.

"I did not. I never stole anything from you. You chased me and I got away."

The police officer looked skeptical.

"We had your kind here in town before, it usually means trouble. Where are the rest of you people?

You folks always come in big groups, you call them caravans, right?"

"I don't live in a caravan anymore. I am married. My husband is Jan Reinhard."

"She's a liar. You know how they are they're all liars. They come into town and steal from the farmers and con our women with their fortune telling."

The police officer licked his lips as he looked at my breasts. Fat jiggled on his sweaty face as I saw him stand straighter. Thick fingers grabbed my arm. I was frightened. We had been taught as children to fear the law. When the police came upon the gypsies, they always came to arrest us or if we were lucky send us on our way. Early on, I knew that as far as the Rom was concerned the law had absolute power. He could do as he wished with me and there would be no one to answer to.

"Please, I never stole anything from these boys. I came to town to find the doctor.'

"Sure and you expect me to believe that?" Fingers twitching his grip on my arm tightened, and I tried to pull away.

"Let me go, please..."

"I don't think so; I think we need to take a deeper look into this situation"

The way he was staring at my body, I knew I was in trouble.

"Please" I begged again, struggling to get away.

A tall slender woman close to my age walked out of a doorway just a few feet in front of us. In the sunlight, her hair was the color of maple syrup and as she turned towards me, I saw that her eyes were golden like liquid honey.

"What's going on here?"

"I'm sorry if we disturbed you, miss, but we have a gypsy girl here causing trouble."

"I'm not causing any trouble. I need to find the doctor, my mother is sick and now these boys are accusing me of stealing and I'm being arrested."

I tugged trying to release his grasp.

"Let her go. I know this girl; she's come to see me."

When she motioned for me to follow the officer's hand went limp.

"My father's a physician. Perhaps, he can help you."

She led me to a building up the street, opened the door and together we walked into a crowded office. People of all ages sat in rows waiting their turn to see the gago medicine man, but she took me in ahead of everyone.

"Father, do you have a moment?"

"Yes dear, always for you. Come into my office."

An ornately carved desk placed in front of a large picture window was the first thing I saw when I entered the doctor's office. A rug of muted colors covered most of the hardwood floor. The doctor motioned for us to sit and we both did.

"Who is your friend?"

"Actually, I don't even know her name, but I heard a commotion outside and when I went out the police were arresting her. It seems she had come into town looking for a medical assistance for her mother."

"So, what is your name, young lady?"

"Zigeuya Reinhard. I need help, sir, because my mother is very sick. It might be a curse that someone put on her, but I don't think so. I tried all the medicine I know. She can no longer walk and needs help to eat. I would have brought her here if I could, but she is unable to travel."

"I see. Where do you live?"

I gave him directions to the farm and he promised me he would visit after finishing the day's patients. In the face of the gago doctor, there was a special light of kindness. That was my first impression of him, and I was right.

When we left the office, the girl introduced herself. "My name is Hannah Stein."

"Thank you, Hannah, for everything."

"I understand the ugliness of hatred and prejudice. My father and I are Jews."

"I guess you know that I am of the Romany, by my clothes, but there is nothing that distinguishes you."

"No, not really, except for the little skull cap my father wears."

I had been so caught up in my own problems I hadn't noticed.

"If you would like, come tonight with your father. My husband taught me to bake strudel. I'll prepare some. You were so kind to me today."

"I'm glad I could help."

I hurried back to my horse; I had left tied to a post a few feet from the building. Watching as a group of men riding bicycles filled the street; I huddled into an alleyway and wondered what it would be like to ride one of those things.

Lucky for me Jan had been too busy to notice I had gone into town. He would have been worried.

By the time, he came back to the house for dinner I had returned.

"The gago doctor is coming tonight. I went to town and found him."

"I'm glad he's coming, but it isn't safe for you to go alone. You should have asked me to take you."

"I know, but I knew you were busy."

"I am never too busy to take care of you. You are so precious to me, love that I would not want anything to happen to you."

"Yes, I know. I do. I just didn't want to be a burden."

"You could never be a burden to me. You are everything that matters, can't you see that?' I nodded.

"I'm glad the doctor is going to look at Mama. I think it's wise."

"She looks bad."

"Don't fret sweetheart, perhaps he will be able to help."

He held me in his arms and feeling his strength, I relaxed. I could not help but think about what could have happened had the girl Hannah not come to my aid.

It was well after nine that evening when the doctor and his daughter arrived by horse and buggy. I showed him to mama's room. When she saw him, my mother's eyes grew wide with fright.

"Who is this man, why is he here?"

Drool dribbled out of the side of her mouth as she spoke with slurred speech.

"Mama, please let him look at you, he's a doctor."

"A gago doctor? No...take him away...no."

Panic shook her body and tremors crept across her face. When he saw this Jan walked over to her bedside and took her hand.

"Mama, please let the doctor look at you. You know that I would never do anything to hurt you. Do it for me?"

My mother's eyes met my husband's sincere ones and she nodded in agreement. Jan amazed me once again.

Dr. Stein insisted that we leave him alone to examine the patient and after Jan smiled at me to let me know it would be alright, I agreed.

The three of us sat in the kitchen in silence, with the strudel on the table untouched, awaiting the results.

It wasn't long before Dr Stein returned.

"Your mother is very ill, what she has cannot be cured. I can give her medicine to make her more comfortable. She will continue to require constant care, I'm afraid."

"Is she dying?" I knew my voice came out as a croak for as much as I had fought with her I loved my mother.

"She could live a long time in her condition. It's hard to say."

I was angry. The gago doctor had proved little more than a waste of time. Unable to voice my distain I walked outside. Hannah followed me. "I'm sorry about your mother. If he could have done anything he would have."

"I know." The anger dissipated and sadness took its place. "Thank you. I just don't know what I'm going to do when she's gone. The thought terrifies me."

"I can understand, in a way. I mean not exactly. My mother died when I was born, but if I ever lost my father I don't know what I'd do."

We shared a bond that day that built into a friendship, one I was hardly expecting. Hannah came to see me often. She brought hard cookies that we dunked into tea as we sat talking for hours. Over the years of living alone with her father, he had come to be very dependent on her. Pretty as she was, I was sure that was why she remained unmarried. Worried that he could not get along without her she kept the house and his books at the office, as well as going to market and preparing meals. Somehow, with all of these responsibilities, she still found time to spend with me, and I was grateful.

With mama, sick things became overwhelming. She

was unable to feed herself and required the use of a chamber pot. Jan, regardless of his own work, helped me daily. He fed mama and emptied her pot while I bathed her and changed her bedding. Most of the time she was depressed and her speech was difficult to understand. I found that I was always tired. Jan took over my responsibilities so I could rest. I felt bad, because he was working so hard himself. But he never complained.

I knew I was pregnant when my bleeding did not come for two months. For two years, Jan and I had been making love constantly and I had not conceived.

The child I carried was Grigori's.

Filled with guilt and anguish I looked at my husband and wondered how I could betray him with this lie. However, when I told him I thought I was pregnant he was so overjoyed that I didn't have the heart to tell him the truth.

Insisting that I not lift anything or do any hard work, he made sure to indulge my every wish and took excellent care of mama.

Desperately wanting to unburden myself I considered telling Hannah about Grigroi. But I was not sure I could make her understand, so I said nothing.

Winter nights were spent watching the fire whirl in shades of orange and red laced with blue. Jan held me in his arms and I discovered the cold weather was my most favorite time of year. I knitted baby clothes and we made plans. Jan built a precious wooden crib, which he painstakingly carved with tiny birds because I said they were good luck. Caught up in the joy of his love I forgot my predicament and convinced myself that we were having the child we had been wishing for.

Thunder crashed through the early morning sky on that cool day in April that you were born. I awakened with a start to find the bed wet. Immediately reminded of the miscarriage I had in Siberia, I touched the area and looked at my hand half expecting to see blood. It was only water. By my side, Jan slept quietly. Not wanting to startle him, I gently shook his arm. His eyes opened slowly.

"I'm having the baby. My water broke."

Sleep left his face and he sprung to life immediately. "I'll get the doc and Hannah too." "What about mama? She needs to eat."

"I'll explain everything to her. Stay in bed. She'll understand. I'll be back as soon as I can." He could ride as well if not better than I could so he would not be gone long. A little past one that afternoon, you were born. I wish you could have seen the look on Jan's face when he held you for the first time. How he loved you. Dr. Stein handed you to him and he beamed with pride as Hannah stood by smiling at me. What a glorious day that was. Together we decided to name you Margot; it was Jan's mother's name.

Two nights after you were born I felt the emptiness on the other side of our bed. I rose to see if everything was alright. I found Jan holding you in his arms and looking out the window as he gently rocked you back to sleep. Quietly I walked over to him and put my arm around his waist. When he looked at me I saw the depth of love in his eyes. Then he leaned over, careful not to wake you, and kissed me.

Mama, although she could not speak, was enraptured with you. Unsteady she shook her head when I asked if she wanted to hold you, instead I held you as she stroked the tiny black curls the stuck to your head. For the first time since her illness began, she looked like she was at peace.

And she was finally, for the next day Mama died.

With a tray of food in my hands I went to her bed, she lay motionless. Without even touching her, I knew she was gone. Mama had lived just long enough to see you come into the world and now she was on her way to be with papa throughout eternity.

I should have been comforted, but I wasn't. I mourned in the Romany style, refusing food and filling myself with alcohol and black coffee.

Concerned with your well-being, Jan intervened. In his tender and understanding way, he tried to convince me to eat. My milk would dry up if I didn't, he told me. I couldn't. Stunned by the realization that I was an orphan, I lay in bed staring blankly at the wall.

One afternoon Hannah came, she recognized my depression and spoke to Jan concerning a wet nurse.

He agreed to take you to the home of a woman who she knew had given birth recently to a stillborn. Twice daily, he hitched up the wagon and took you, as I lay prostrated with grief. Until one morning, the wet nurse came to our house. Because I wanted to meet her, I forced myself out of bed. She was a buxom blond, with skin the color of crab apples. From the doorway, I watched her cradle you in her arms and put you to her naked breast. Jan stood beside her; neither of them realized I was watching. She looked up at him and smiled. The woman's face told me that she found my husband attractive, far too much so.

That night when he came to bed, for the first time since mama died I kissed him. Taking me in his arms he held me lovingly.

"That woman that was here today? The wet nurse."

"Yes."

"What do you think of her?"

"She's a nice lady. I was glad she was able to help us."

"And do you find her pretty? Do you want her?"

He laughed.

"No, there is no other woman for me. Not now, not ever. You are my wife. From the first time I saw you sitting in the middle of my field stealing strawberries, what you actually stole was my heart. I married you and I vowed to love and cherish you for all of my life, and I do and I will. You are the only woman I will ever want, you can count on that. I could never be unfaithful to you. I would never have the desire. You are and always will be everything I need."

Disgusted with myself as a quick memory of that single moment when I had wanted Grigori flashed through my mind. I squeezed my eyes shut and with great effort, I willed it away.

Early the following morning I got out of bed, washed up, cleaned the house and began to be a mother to you.

The next ten years were the best of my entire life. You were a mild mannered little girl with a vivid imagination. Our little family lay sprawled out under a tree watching the clouds. I'd packed a picnic lunch because Jan liked to be with you as much as possible. After we ate, we did some cloud gazing you told me what you saw in the sky.

"Look mama, that one is a dog with a big snout."

"What do you see over there?" Jan would ask as he pointed to a cloud formation that looked like a star.

"I don't know papa, is that a real star or a cloud?"

"It's anything you want it to be sweetheart. Anything at all." For Christmas one year, Jan built you a rocking horse. Until you were too big, you played on it every day. He carved you dolls and I made the clothes for them.

We taught you to ride a horse and milk a cow. From Jan you learned to read, and he spent many winter nights by the fire reading you fairy tales. I told you stories of the Rom and our travels and our lives in the Kompanias. But you were most fascinated by Dr. Stein. You loved the gago medicine, even then. With the herbs in our garden, I showed you the healings of our people, but you longed to be a doctor not a medicine woman. Hannah took you to her father's office. The older man enjoyed your enthusiasm and so he allowed you to help him out.

As soon as you got home, you ran into your father's arms. He lifted you high in the air and called you his angel. Then he swung you around until you were both laughing so hard that I had to put a stop to it so that you didn't get dizzy. After he put you down, you told him proudly of your accomplishments that day. "Papa, I set a broken arm," or "Dr. Stein let me help him sew up a cut on a man's finger." For an entire year, you begged us for a pet. An animal that could live inside the house, you said. Against my better judgment, I allowed Jan to convince me to get a dog. I know you must remember "Spritz."

The Zellman's had these little brown and white pups. To surprise you, early one morning while you were still asleep, Jan took the buggy and rode over to their farm. I don't know how much money it cost him, but when he pulled that tiny dog with a face all wrinkled up like an old man out of your yellow baby blanket we all fell in love. You ran through the house screaming with delight as the puppy followed you with its tail wagging wildly. We let you name him and you decided on "Spritz."

A surprising addition to our family, the animal became a true friend. And, I must admit, I came to love that loyal creature dearly.

They say that marriage takes the passion out of love. It was not so with us. Our love began like a flower and blossomed into an entire garden. Never once did our lovemaking seem old or routine. As soon as you fell asleep we, lay together absorbed in the intimacy only years together can bring. But in the back of my mind, I remained haunted by the truth that I had never shared with him. The influenza hit us hard, the year that you were ten. You must remember having it. Your slender shoulders racked with a dry cough that took your breath away. Jan stayed up all night with you, and he could not be lured from your side to rest. Even when I told him to sleep, that I would stay with you he would not go. Occasionally dozing by your bedside he wanted to be there in case you woke up and called for him. Dr. Stein and Hanna came often and provided you with medicine. Slowly you got better.
One night your father started coughing. I lit the candle by the bed and he was covered in a red rash. Rain poured from the sky that night, but I took Mara and rode to Dr. Stein's house. Hannah answered the door and knew immediately that

something was wrong. She feared you had relapsed, but I explained it wasn't you, but Jan who was ill.

The doctor followed me back to our farm. His clothes soaking wet when he arrived, he did not stop to dry off. Instead, he went to the bedroom your father and I shared.

He offered medicine, and told me to watch him and see how he did.

Jan' grew weak. I tried all of the medicine I knew, but to no avail.

Agonized but left with no other choice, I found a messenger and offered him a good sum to go to Petrograd and find Rasputin.

I had heard that Grigori was living in the court of the Romanov's now. He was the only one who could heal the heir to the dynasty. Tales circulated that there was a curse on the child, where upon he bled and could not stop bleeding. Grigori was the only one who could stop the flow of blood. Rumors spread like wild fire throughout Europe of the mad monk who was a miraculous healer, and the power he had over Alexandria the Czarina of Russia. Without him, it was said, the boy Alexi would surely die. There had been talk of an attempt on his life by a prostitute who he had treated poorly. Everyone said he was magic, because she cut his stomach open, in a surprise attack, spilling his insides all over the street.

Against miraculous odds he did not die. He could not be killed, they said.

Of course, I knew it to be true, and I knew why. He still wore my blessing and as long as he did, he was protected from harm. He could not be killed.

I asked Hannah to write a letter for me begging Grigori to come and help my husband. Kindly she refrained from asking me any questions, and I was relieved that she did. Please, I implored him you are my only hope. Then I sent the letter by messenger.

When a week had passed and I received no answer I found another person and sent off another letter.

This time I would pay only upon his return with an answer from Grigori.

It was two weeks and I was frantic. Jan's condition was growing worse by the day. His body burned with fever so I tried to cool his forehead with wet cloths.

Dr. Stein tried every medicine he knew. Although he was helpless, the doctor and Hannah arrived at the farm every other night to check on Jan's condition.

I stayed by Jan's side, waiting for Grigori. I knew, beyond a doubt, he could save my husband. In the letter, I offered him any sum of money that he wanted, and I would gladly have paid.

On a Tuesday evening, the messenger returned.

"I'm sorry, ma'am. I saw Rasputin and he refuses to come. He says to tell you that you sent him away and he has no intentions of helping you or your husband. I hate to give you this news and I hope you'll still pay me."

My throat closed up and I couldn't answer. Nodding, I gave him a handful of coins. Satisfied, he   left. I sunk into the chair at Jan's bedside.

Every day he suffered and I knew he was slipping away from me, and there was nothing I could do to save him. I would have gone to the medicine woman, but I was afraid he would die while I was gone. I dared not leave him for a moment.

On my knees I prayed, I begged God to let him live. Take me instead I bargained over and over but God was not listening.

When I knew the end was coming, guilt filled me so strongly that I could not fight the need to tell him.

I grasped his hand in both of mine and looked into those eyes that had brought me out of pain and into such love and joy as I could never have imagined.

Tears filled the back of my eyes.

"Jan, there's something I must tell you." I could barely speak, but I knew I had to go on. "Ten years ago. Grigori came back and you were in town and mama was asleep and Oh God, Jan forgive me please...."

The tears flooded down my face like a river.

"I should have told you sooner, but I ..."

Gently he placed his cold hand over my lips and looked into my eyes.

The deep aqua of his eyes where I had seen joy and love so often, was now glazed, his face was serious as he said...

Chapter Eleven

"Shhh" his voice barely audible. "It's okay, love, I already know."

Unable to control the trembling, I watched the man who had been my husband and dearest friend, slipping away from me. He deserved to know the truth. My throat went dry, as I removed his hand from my lips.

"Jan, Margot is Grigori's child." I told him.

Margot, I am sorry that I had to tell you this, but it is necessary for your future that you know. Jan's answer was the most beautiful thing anyone has ever said to me. "She is my child. I raised her and I love her." That smile that comforted me as no other came over his face. "I knew about Grigori, but never for one day have I felt that she belonged to anyone else. She may not be of my blood, but she carries my heart. As soon as Dr. Stein put that little girl in my arms, she became my daughter, our daughter."

"I'm so sorry, Jan. I never meant to hurt you. I don't know if it matters, but that was the only time I betrayed you"

"Please, love, I have no regrets. You've made my life so much more than I could ever have hoped for.

You have always been my angel, my reason for living and whatever happened makes no difference. I love you, I always have, and I always will."

For a brief second, the light came back into his eyes. Through my tears, I watched and hoped against hope that he was coming back to me.

"Please, God, don't take him. I'll do anything, anything."

He winked and touched my face one last time, and although it was strained, he smiled that old familiar smile, closed his eyes, and was gone.

It was early December and a light coat of virgin snow had fallen the previous night. I gazed out the window to see the morning sunlight sprinkling down in a rainbow of diamonds across the pure white powder.

My heart was as empty, as if someone had cut it out leaving a big hole that was bleeding through my entire body. Glued to the bed looking at his lifeless body, I was terrified.

You ran into the room with Sprite wagging his tail right behind you. You called to me. "Mama, Mama, can I have some cookies?"

You stopped when you saw me and your little face turned pale as you ran into my arms. When you saw your father was dead, you cried in such heart, wrenching sobs that your entire body turned blood red. Unable to catch your breath, you vomited on the floor.

We buried him on a Sunday. Paralyzed with grief, I stood at the gravesite holding your hand. Icicles hung from the trees and occasionally fell to the ground. My ears froze but I couldn't feel the pain. My eyes were dry, but the ache that had started in my heart now filled my stomach and throat as well.

Your father had so many friends; he had gone out of his way to help others as long as I had known him.

And now people came to me with their condolences, but I couldn't hear them when they spoke. I longed to be alone. Even Hannah was no comfort to me.

Weeks passed and I did not eat, only drank alcohol, until in a drunken stupor, I slept. You tried to come to me, but I sent you away.

Hannah came to stay with us, but her own responsibilities forced her to go home. She begged me to go with her, but I wouldn't move from the bed I had shared with your father. Wisely, she begged me to allow her to take you to her home, and I agreed.

For a few hours at a time, I would be fine. It would be as if nothing had happened, and then I would see something as simple as Jan's coat or his shoes and the pain would come over me with a vengeance. My mind drifted back to the strawberry patch when we first met. How I had taken him for a fool. Laughing bitterly to myself, I realized it was I who had been the fool; he was a gift from God to me.

When we were newly married, I remembered how he laughed and teased me as I braided garlic and hung it over our door to ward off evil spirits. When he saw how serious I was, he stopped laughing and helped me to make the protective talisman. Jan, always so wise.

I buried my face in his clothes breathing deeply trying to suck every bit of essence left of him into my body. So great was my sorrow that I fell to the ground and cried out his name, over and over until I was hoarse and could no longer make any sound. All of my strength drained, I wept quietly. Jan had been the only person who could ever pull me out of depths of my sadness, and now it was him that I grieved for. For the first time, I realized how much I had leaned on him. He had been my strength. Sheer exhaustion came over me and I slept.

Deeper than I had ever slept before. It was as if I had left this world for a while. Jan came to me in a dream and begged me not to give up. He implored me to be a mother to you. His face was as close as mine is to yours now. I believe he came from the other side to help me as he always had in life. I felt his touch, and the spicy fragrance of his skin filled the room. He would always be with me by my side in spirit guiding me as I walked through life until the time we would be together again. Waiting with open arms, he said, he would be there to catch me when my time came to leave this earth. His lips were warm and tender on mine, and for the first time since he died, I was comforted.

When I awoke, I felt stronger and I made a decision. I would devote my life to raising you, but first I had something important that I needed to do.

I pulled the black valise from the back of the closet and packed a few things, filled a small purse with money, and left. I walked over to the farm next door and asked if they would take care of our animals for a few weeks. Once I had arranged things, I was on my way.

I had a debt to pay.

So filled with anxiety, I felt pin pricks in my fingers as I took the coins from my velvet money purse to pay the man at the ticket booth in the train station.

With his thick black hair graying at the temples and pushed down under his hat, he asked me,

"Where're ya going?'

"Petrograd," I answered.

Thinking to myself, (to the court of the Romanov's to find Grigori Rasputin).

Chapter Twelve

In the wee hours of a frigid morning, on the 29th of December in the year of 1916, I arrived in Petrograd. After a long and exhausting journey, I was tired and famished. But I had a mission and would not rest until it was complete.

Before I left the train, with its foul odors and uncomfortable seats, I asked directions to the Winter Palace of the Romanovs. Carefully, I listened and committed to memory all that I heard. Then, disembarking onto the platform, I felt the remembered chill of the frozen Russian winter. Forceful winds blew as I took my suitcase and began my journey.

Excruciating pain from the cold shot through my toes like tiny bullets, as I made my way on foot to the palace.

Deserted, the silent streets stretched before me. The icy chill bit my nose. Water dripped from my eyes, freezing on my lashes. I rubbed my already blistering hands together in an effort to warm them. I arrived several hours later. Leafless trees adorned with snow surrounded the Palace. A huge structure, golden in the sun, appeared to go on for miles, with rows of more windows than I had ever seen. A tall column stood before the castle. There was a statue at the top wearing wings like an angel.

I must have looked very out of place, because I was immediately approached by a guard with a black thick mustache, similar to the ones worn by the Romany men. He wanted to know my purpose for being there. I asked to see Grigori Rasputin.

A vulgar knowing laugh sprung from his lips, causing my face to go scarlet.

"Another village girl looking for the amorous monk? Well, I am truly sorry, little miss, but I can't admit anyone who is not of the court."

Turning his back on me, he started to walk away. Filled with desperation, I called out to him, "Sir, kind sir, please...you must listen to me."

Without turning, he continued on his way. Panic filled my mind. I realized that after all of this travel I might not be admitted to the palace at all. The thought of returning home without seeing Grigori infuriated me. I had to think of something...

Final Chapter

"Sir, I can offer you money. Plenty of money. I will pay you whatever you ask. I must see Rasputin." His thick rigid body turned at a perfect right angle to face me. A heavy coat the color of red bricks sheltered him from the cold.

"Money, you say? How much?"

A sparkle of greed in his eyes indicated: that for the right price he would take me to Grigori.

Negotiations began. With half my life savings spent on a single bribe, I entered the palace.

I was dumbstruck by the majesty of it. Illuminated by crystal chandeliers that hung heavily from the ceilings, the large rooms dwarfed me. Pictures of the Romanov family hung in brushed gold frames on the ivory colored walls. The heels of the guard's boots as they hit the black and cream checkered marble floor echoed as only sound in an otherwise soundless palace. As he led me along, I saw a staircase so magnificent that it stopped me for a moment. It curved around on two sides with white carved banisters, meeting in the center to form a high balcony. Painstakingly perfect carvings of vines adorned the entire area. I gasped in awe.

Poking my back with his elbow, the guard looked around to be sure we had not been seen in the palace. Then, turning back, he looked at me "Move along now, there is no time to stand around."

He took my arm and pulled me forward.

"Move along now."

The guard noticed I had stopped and in fear for his job, he wanted to hurry me out of sight. I followed quickly without a word.

My heart pounded so loudly I feared he would hear it as we made our way through the endless rooms up to an antechamber. With a hard knock on the door, not waiting for an answer, the guard turned the handle and bid me enter. Then, leaving me on my own, he walked away. My knees trembled as I came into the hall.

In the center of the large open area, surrounded by elegantly dressed women, Grigori sat on a plush golden colored velvet chair. His hands gestured and his smile warmly charmed the ladies who gazed at him spellbound.

When he saw me standing in the doorway, his face grew dark. His features twisted into a grimace that broke into a smirk. Then a look of amusement took over. "Well, well, well, what brings you here, my little gypsy? And how, dare I ask, did you get in?"

I glared at him for a moment. "You bring me here, Grigori."

"Oh, so finally you miss me? Perhaps it is far too late for that."

"Perhaps it is, but I would like to speak with you, alone."

"Excuse me ladies, this is an old friend from a time long past."

Breezing past me, his black robe floating around him, he walked outside the door. I followed.

"So, my little flower, say that you missed me."

"Of course, Grigori. I missed you." The words tasted like bitter bile on my lips.

"Hmm, we did have some lovely times, did we not?'

I nodded, unable to speak.

His eyes penetrated my clothes and I was sure his memory reconstructed a time when he had shared my bed. Licking his lips, he considered how to go forward. Silent for several minutes, he seemed lost in thought. Then a look of confidence came over him and he smiled.

"Tonight I have an appointment with a Princess at the Moika Palace, one I must keep, I am afraid. However, a midnight rendezvous would be a pleasant change from all of these stuffy court ladies. You always were quite the lover, my dear."

He took my hand and pressed it to his lips.

"I will be dining with the Yusupov's and I am sure that if you go to the kitchen at their palace they will find work for you- cleaning perhaps. Then, when the dinner is done, I will find you. One of these ladies," he gestured to the women who awaited his return in the antechamber, "will do me the favor of driving you over. However, you must not speak of our intended meeting. Tell them you are an old friend of mine who has come to me in hopes of my finding work for you."

Amazed at his arrogance, I nodded in agreement.

Satisfied with my response, he arranged for a ride and before I knew it I was on my way. The palace of the Yusupov's, small compared to the Romanov's, smacked of elegance. Off to the kitchen I went, and requested a day's work in exchange for a meal. The head cook, a large boned woman of undetermined age, with a light dusting of hair on her thick chins, agreed. I would be required to dust and shine all of the floors. Instead of making me finish my work first, out of pity, she fed me right away. Until I began eating, I did not realize the extent of my hunger. As I ate, I overheard her and another cook deep in conversation.

"Look at all this food and wine. The master insisted I order so much. Rather kindly, he said we could each have a plate before the guests arrive."

"This is so odd for the master to have a dinner party while the princess is out of town." "I can't recall him ever doing it before. The wife has always been present at his dinners in the past. Who is to be attending?"

"Only one I am sure of is Grigori Rasputin. I think there will be others but I don't know who they are."

"Have you ever seen him?'

"Rasputin?"

"Yes"

"No, never, but I hear he has magical powers and all women fall in love with him."

"I haven't either and I don't care if I never see him. The master says that when all the food is prepared you and I can have the rest of the night off."

"That would be nice for a change."

"Quite frankly, I can't wait. A nice evening to myself, how grand. We aren't even required to serve; he says he can manage alone. That's a pleasant change. Come on, hurry, let's get this work done so we can leave"

The entire day, I dusted, washed, and shined the floors of the palace. Grigori arrived a little after sunset. I looked up from where I'd been kneeling on the hard marble to see him saunter past. Turning back for just a moment as he was escorted to a private chamber, he winked at me. My back, knees, and shoulders ached with the strain of the day's workload. When I tried to stand up straight, for a few moments, I found it to be difficult.

Sympathetic, due to the fierce temperatures outside, the head cook, a kind woman at heart, allowed me to sleep by the fire in the kitchen for the night. Her eyes shone with sympathy as she handed me a blanket. Then she and the other cook prepared to leave the palace for the night. Jovial at the prospect of an evening to themselves, the two cooks made their way out of the building, but not before offering me a plate of food.

After a filling dinner of chicken tabka with fried panisse and seared sweetbreads, taken from the dinner preparations, I lay down on a thick wool carpet of swirling bright colors. Surrounded by the wholesome smell of food and the warmth of the fire, my weary body eased. I watched the flames leap and dance and was transported to the night I had danced before the fire for Jan so long ago. Heavy eyed, I allowed myself to drift into a deep slumber. Resting comfortably for the first time in several days, my sleep felt like a drunken stupor. I did not realize how long I had slept until I heard a gunshot that woke me abruptly. From the room that Grigori had entered, where the party had taken place, I heard three distinctive men's voices, one of them with a British accent. They shouted, more gunshots rang out, and I sat up looking around. A loud hammering echoed through the halls as if someone were tearing down the palace. Cries of pain trumpeted alerting of a terrible suffering. Curling into myself, I hid in a corner behind the cast iron stove and listened.

"He's still not dead. I shot him in the head, I've attacked him with this club, and still he lives. Nothing seems to affect him"

"Beat him again."

"I have again and again; he is a bloody mess, yet he does not die."

"Grab the rug over there, If we wrap him in it he will be easier to transport. Then we can take him and throw him into the Neva River. Freezing him will kill him. No one could survive that. Not even this bloody bastard."

"Watch out for him, he tried to take hold of me."

"How can that be? Together we've shot him four times and still he is fighting back and trying to get away. Any normal man would have died."

"Any other man would have died from all of the cyanide I put into that food and wine he ate. It was enough to kill five men."

"And still he lives."

From the strain in their voices, I knew they struggled to wrap him in the rug. From my hiding place, I watched as they dragged his body out. I knew instinctively that it was Rasputin they were trying to murder. I did not want the men to know I had been a witness, lest they decide it best to destroy any evidence. After all, I knew how beloved Grigori was by the royal family. So I peeked from behind the stove and waited. Then, once sure that everyone had gone, I followed in the shadows as they took him to the banks of the Neva River

Because Grigori had been such a large and imposing man, it took all three of them to hoist the body into the water. They waited for a few minutes to be sure their task was complete. But the bitter weather forced them to tighten their coats, and with the wind at their backs, they left. Once they turned the corner and I could no longer see them, I knew it would be safe to come out. Standing at the edge of the half-frozen water, I watched Grigori struggle as he freed himself from the wrap. His eyes met mine.

"Help me, please Zigeuya , my one true love, help me."

"Your one true love, Grigori? You killed my one true love. I begged you, but you would not come and so I lost the only man who ever cared for me. You have a child, a daughter. He raised and cared for her as his own, more than you would ever have done."

"How can you say that? I love you I have always loved you."

"Grigori, you killed my one true love and now I will kill the only person you have ever loved...yourself."

"Please, be reasonable...help me, you will come to live in the palace, bring our child. I will take care of you." For one brief moment, the old feelings tried to surface, but I pushed them down. Raising my hand and pointing my two fingers at him as the wind whipped my hair about my face in a wicked icy dance, I said, "I remove my protection from you now, Grigori Rasputin. You are no more than a mortal   man."

Changed instantly by the reversal of the spell, he was now affected by the gunshots, poison, and frozen water. The strength drained from his body and he became weak and vulnerable.

Tears filled my eyes as I watched him sink beneath the dark waters of the river. For several seconds, seeming like hours, he stared at me as he struggled against the filling of his lungs. Then he lay still, his black eyes open and fixed upon me forever.

Grigori Rasputin, my first lover, the man whose seed I had carried, my enemy, and my rival, was dead.

I spent the remainder of the night in the train station. The following morning, I found myself heading back to Munich and to you.

As you know, over the next ten years we became as one. You are my daughter and my best friend. I have loved you and will always love you. I am pleased that Dr Stein willed that money to you for your education. Go as planned to Oxford and become a doctor. And now we come to the reason why I needed to tell you this story. My child, you have your father's gift. It is in your hands; you have the power to save the dying. Use it wisely, but take care that no one ever finds out the truth about your paternity. There are many who still hate Rasputin and who feel that he was the downfall of Russia. If they ever realize who you are, I fear they will kill you.

Take care my child, my dear sweet Margot, and know always that your father and I loved you with all of our hearts.

"Mama, stop...please...you are not ready to die. I can postpone my leaving for school and stay with you. You say I have the gift, - then I will lay hands upon you. I will save you."

"No child, I want to go, yearn to go. My work here is complete. I've raised you into an incredible young woman. It is now time to see your father. He has waited long enough and I ache to be with him. Your life is ahead of you, your dreams and your future await...go...fly my little bird...take your wings and fly."

Turning her head away, the old gypsy witch closed her eyes on the world for the last time. Jan smiled that old familiar smile, his blond hair falling over his eyes, as he waited with open arms on the other side. She ran to him, and was instantly turned a young girl again. All of the disease and hardship of her life on earth dissolved in a cloud of fairy dust. Laughing as her skirts blew wildly, he lifted her off the ground in a long awaited embrace. Their lips met as their hearts and bodies joined together   for   eternity.
Outside the window, a rainbow peeked though the silver white clouds. Margot smiled as a single tear fell from her eyes onto the pillow. Then she left the

room to pack her bags for school. After the funeral and the sale of the farm, she would take the train to England and into her future...

If you enjoyed "The Gypsy Witch," please visit www.RobertaKagan.com for news and upcoming releases by Roberta Kagan. Join the email list and have a free short story emailed to you!

A note from the author:

"I always enjoy hearing from my readers. Your feelings about my work are very important to me. Please contact me via Facebook or at www.RobertaKagan.com. All emails are answered personally, and I would love to hear from you."

*Continue on to next page to discover
more work by Roberta Kagan*

The Heart of a Gypsy

If you liked "Inglourious Basterds," Pulp Fiction," "Django Unchained," You'll love "The Heart of a Gypsy!"
During the Nazi occupation, bands of freedom fighters roamed the forests of Eastern Europe. They hid, while waging their own private war against Hitler's tyrannical and murderous reign. Among these Resistance Fighters, there were several groups of Romany people (gypsies).
The Heart of a Gypsy is a spellbinding love story. It is a tale of a man with remarkable courage and the woman who loved him more than life itself. This historical novel is filled with romance, and spiced with the beauty of the Gypsy culture.
Within these pages lies a tale of a people who would rather die, than surrender their freedom. Come; enter into a little known world, where only a few have traveled before... The world of the Romany.
If you enjoy romance, secret magical traditions, and riveting action....you will love "The Heart of A Gypsy."
Please be forewarned that this book contains explicit scenes of a sexual nature.

CPSIA information can be obtained
at www.ICGtesting.com
Printed in the USA
LVHW091124131219
640280LV00011B/1181/P